SIAMESE FOLKTALES

Narrated in English by
J. Kasem Sibunruang
with illustrations by
Saeng Aroon Rataksikorn

WILDSIDE PRESS

Volume 1

Printed in Thailand
at Don Bosco Technical School & Orphanage
Bangkok

To my brother
Charoon Sibunruang
Whose understanding, guidance
and support, I am always grateful for.

CONTENTS

PREFACE

Here, in this little book by Mrs. Kasem Sibunruang, are to be found five Thai folktales which are
well-known ones among the mass of the Thai people.
It is a fact that much can be gleaned from folktales
as to the early belief and customs of the people which
have survived among the folk. The Thai people whose
earlier home during historical time was in Southern
China came in contact with Hindu civilization, when
they became a paramount race in the central part
of the Indu China Peninsular. They absorbed much
of this Hindu culture, but as is peculiar to their race,
the Thai people adapted such culture into their own
pattern and tradition as suitable to their own tempera-
ment. Before they adopted Buddhism as a system of
their belief, the Thai, not unlike other people in their
earlier phase of belief, were predominantly animistic.
Such a belief becomes mixed in a degree to the adopted
Buddhism in its popular side. To understand the psy-
chology of the people at large, is to study their belief
and custom as embedded as a survival in many of

their folktales. In Buddhist literature, there is a collection of folktales which is well known as the Famous Jataka Tales or Buddhist Birth Stories. Here, apart from this Jataka Tales, of which many are popularly known, there is another collection of Jataka Tales, particularly known as Pannas Jataka or fifty Jataka Tales. This collection of Buddhist tales, though an apocryphal one, is very interesting to students of folklore. Some of these tales may be traced to their original sources from the Buddhist literature, either Hinayana, of the southern school, or Mahayana, the Northern School. Some of them are perhaps indigenous tales with a touch of Buddhism. Such tales are a store house of the lore people, which may be compared profitably with those of the Thai neighbours.

One of the five tales, the country of the Bird Women is identical substantially with one of the original Jataka Tales, the Sudhana Jataka. It is a tale well known and very popular in the Southern part of the Country down the Malay Peninsular. It forms parts of the popular dramatic performance of the region called Nora. a word corrupted from Manohara, the name of the Bird woman in the tale. One of the other tales is the "Eyes of the Twelve Queens" which is deemed to be the first episode of Nora, and the former tale is considered the sequal. The latter though well known generally, finds its popularity in the East and North Eastern Regions. No doubts, the Lao of the Lao Kingdom and the Cambodians know this story too. I many times have heard the story narrated by many a matron to their children, but find variations in its details with local settings and beliefs peculiar to the regions.

I hope the tales translated will give a further light apart from the entertainment they give, on the culture of the Thai, especially in their earlier time of civilization.

Sthira Koses,

Bangkok, 22 Sept. 54.

Author's Note

These stories were written a few years ago, when my baby daughter began to demand fairy tales at her bed time. I told her what my mother told me, until my stock was exhausted. It came to my mind then that other mothers in my case would appreciate having some stories in reserve, which they would fashion in their own ways for their children. With that thought I began to put some of the original stories I heard on papers. I showed them to H.H. Prince Prem Puracha-tra, who was kind enough to publish them in his weekly newspaper "The Standard"

When Mr. Saeng Aroon Ratakasikorn (M. Arch. Cornell) came back from the United States, he urged me to publish these tales in book form and promised to illustrate them for me.

So here is the book in your hand. It has no pretention to be a translation of the heavy-paged and beautifully-rhymed Jataka, nor a study of our folklore. It is simply what we generally know, as far as Siamese folktales are concerned, and we are glad to share these tales with other people who may be interested in the way of life in this part of the world.

J. Kasem Sibunruang,
Bangkok, 22 September, 1954.

Villa Sivadon,
1,Convent Road,
Bangkok, Thailand.

THE GOLDEN GOBY[1]

This is a story of Siamese origin, based on the animistic belief of reincarnation and punishment for sins committed in one's past life. The story tells of the perpetual feud between an unfortunate daughter and a scheming step-mother, with its direful consequences.

---

1. A small fish with ventral fins joined into a disk sucker.

"FATHER, how is it that you are so late?....And where is Mother?" asked Uay, when she saw her father coming back alone from fishing. But her father did not answer her; he did not even look at her, but went directly to his second wife's quarters, where soon Uay heard him laughing and joking with his two other daughters.

The fisherman, Sethi,[1] had two wives, of whom the first, Kanitha, had a daughter called Uay.[2] The second wife, called Kanithi, had two daughters, Ay[3] and Ee.[4]

For several days, the husband had had many things he wanted to discuss with his second wife and had resented the constant presence of his first wife. Then, the previous day, the two wives had quarrelled and the husband had reprimanded the first wife rather severely. But the next morning, in order that the second wife should not be too proud of her victory, he took the first wife along with him when he went out fishing. But in spite of his good will and his sense of justice, her presence weighed upon him.

---

1. Sethi = rich.   2. Uay = eldest sister.   3. Ay = elder.   4. Ee = younger sister

It came to pass that, on that day, he caught nothing but a tiny little goby. "This woman brings me ill luck", thought the fisherman, and he threw the fish away.

"Please, do not throw it away! I'd like to take it back to my child", said Kanitha, but the husband did not say anything.

Presently the same fish came into the net again, and again the husband threw it away. Seeing that it was the same fish he had caught, Kanitha again asked her husband to keep it, saying:

"You see, my husband, this fish wants to come with us," and she laughed, suspecting not the hatred the man felt against her. "After all, we are not so well off, we never can offer a toy for our child. This fish costs you nothing, and still you refuse it..."

It was a hot day and the fishing was fruitless... "Why does this ungrateful woman reproach me so?", thought the angry fisherman and he struck her with all his strength. The struggle did not last long; Kanitha missed her footing and fell into the water.

"Pah! feminine tactics!", said the furious husband to himself, shrugging his shoulders.

Tired, angry with everything and especially with himself, the fisherman did not attempt to save his wife at all. He started home.... "After all, good riddance to bad rubbish, there will be no more quarrelling under my roof...."

"But, Father, where is Mother?", asked the unfortunate Uay. To these repeated questions, the father finally replied:

"Listen, my child, think well, and stop bothering me with your silly questions:

To a beautiful palace under the sea
Has gone thy mother away from thee.
Come, dost thou not give way to weeping,
In three days' time she will float back sleeping''·

At this instant, the daughter of the first wife realised the truth, she understood the sinister sense of the riddle; she had heard that when one is drowned, the body sinks down first, then floats on the surface for three days, then sinks again. She also knew that the corpse of a woman floats on its back while that of a man floats face downwards.

The poor girl insisted no more. She cried silently over her fate and lamented her mother's death. Scoldings and whippings from her father and especially from her stepmother she endured bravely. Outraged, but resigned, Uay ceased to give way to her grief. She bore the cruel yoke silently.

Now that Uay was deprived of her mother, she had to do all the hard work for the whole household. But she hurried through her work without complaint. As soon as she had a spare moment, she would run to the river. But, alas, nothing was to be seen. Days passed and there was no sign of her mother.

One day, as Uay was looking into the clear water, she saw a strange little fish; it glittered under the water, as if made of gold. Uay wiped her tears away, and for the first time diverted from her grief, she spoke aloud: "My poor little fish, I wish I had something to give you to eat...." To her great astonishment, she heard the fish say: "My little Mouse,[1] I am your Mother.... Listen to me and try to understand: I was killed cruelly, so the gods showed mercy and have granted me the power of speech...."

According to superstition, the last vision before death has an influence upon the form one takes in the next reincarnation. Kanitha's thought was fixed upon the goby; so once dead, she took the form of a goby.

Uay's gladness knew no bounds. She took the fish in her hands, fondled her and told her all the details of her wretched life. But time was short, Uay had to run home lest her absence should be noticed. At night she crept into the garden and dug a little pond.... You can never tell, you can never be too sure of the current.. nor of the fisher's net....and the thought had filled her with anguish.....

Now that Uay had taken the fish into her pond she was almost happy again; she came to feed her and spent long hours playing with and talking to her mother...

Now Uay had a new job: she had to take care of the ducks; she had had no rice for her fish, so she

---

1. Mouse - an intimate term of endearment.

reserved the tender morsels which were given her for
the ducks.

Unhappily, one day, her step-sisters caught her
speaking into the pond, and they duly reported to their
mother, who guessed the truth and ordered her elder
daughter Ay to catch the fish. The mother then sent
Uay to look after the cows near the forest. Uay was sad
and worried. What would happen to her golden goby
during a whole day's absence? She fidgeted uncomfor-
tably all day long, asking the animals not to wander too
far off: she would like to get home as soon as she could.
The animals understood her entreaties and stayed within
sight.

In the meantime, Kanithi and her daughers took
the fish out of the pond and prepared a delicious dish
which they ate triumphantly. They took care to get rid
of all traces. They gave the hones to their cats and the
rest was thrown into the river. However, while they
were preparing the fish, one of the scales fell to the
ground. A duck saw it and picked it up for Uay who had
been so kind to him.

Uay hurried home when the sun was low in the
west. She ran to the pond and called her goby, but in
vain. Desperate, she went to her pet animals. The dogs
and the cats looked at her silenty. But the gods had
mercy on her and allowed the duck to have the power
of speech, not only did it give her the scale, but also
told her the whole story....

Grieved and bewildered, Uay bore her sorrow silently. She went about her work humbly, taking care not to show her feelings. She was resigned to her fate now; she put the beloved scale in a corner of her handkerchief and it consoled her to feel it next to her heart. One day she took the cows further than usual into the forest; there was a quite, peaceful spot that pleased her a great deal. "I shall bury mother's relic here" said Uay to herself. "It is far from the house and nobody would think to come and harm it". Thus she buried the fish scale there and felt much better for having laid it to rest.

Now she was quite content to go about her work. She took the animals to the forest as soon as the house work was done. That seeming contentment, faint as it was, puzzled the step-mother and she sent her two daughters to spy on Uay.

Days and weeks went by, and it came to pass that at the spot where Uay had her mother's little tomb, there grew two plants called Makheua Proh.[1] These two plants, with their thick green leaves, bore a great quantity of fruit. The joy of the motherless Uay knew no bounds. But, alas, it was short-lived, for soon her two sisters found the plants and uprooted them, eating the fruit and throwing the rest into the river.

---

1.   a kind of egg-plant, with delicious green fruit and hard seeds.

Here was more sorrow for the poor girl. She asked no questions, she did not even cry, but sat dumbly under the "sai"[1] tree. Silent, patient, her young heart heavy with pain and disappointment, she watched the cows grazing. The animals had pity on her; they never went out of her sight and their silent presence kept her company. But when it was time to take the animals home, Uay cringed at the thought of facing the cruelty of her step-mother and the two other girls. Her father took no part in the game. He had washed his hands of the whole business; but his very silence hurt Uay's affectionate young heart.

To her surprise, she had one friend; it was the duck. It followed Uay everywhere. When Uay went to the river to wash the dishes, she found the duck by her side, and as soon as they were alone, the duck gave Uay some of the Makheua seeds she had kept in her beak and told Uay about the whole incident.

The next day, when Uay took the cattle to the woods, she went a little further and buried the seeds .... She left the place reluctantly and after a few steps looked back. Lo! there stood at the very spot two beautiful papal trees.[2] One of the trees had golden leaves and the other silver ones. Uay came back to them, put her scarf on the fertile soil, and made obeisance over it three times: to her, this was doubly sacred.

---

1. banyan.
2. The papal tree under which Buddha meditated and found the Noble Truths. it is a sacred tree.

Now a king named Thao Phrommathat[1] came to hunt in the forest and saw the beautiful papal trees in this deserted spot. He thought that somebody must have been taking care of them, and ordered inquiries to be made. Thus Uay, young and beautiful, was brought into the royal presence.

The monarch fell in love with her and, not long afterwards, Uay became his queen.

The king graciously ordered that the trees be transported to the palace; but in spite of every effort, even with the help of elephants, it was impossible to move these sacred trees. Uay then prostrated herself on the very ground in front of the trees, saluted three times and said in her heart. "My mother, if you refuse to go to the palace, I will not leave you. These trees are all that I possess in this world. Please hear me, and answer my prayer." She then took hold of the trees with both hands, and out of the ground they came....

This was the most happy period in Uay's life so far. Unfortunately, it did not last long. Her step-mother heard about her new life and worked out a plan with the aid of a witch, for she meant to make her own daughter queen at all costs.

Accordingly, Kanithi sent for Uay, pretending that her father had been taken very seriously ill. Suspecting nothing, Uay hurried to her old home. She was met

1. Brahma data

by her step-mother at the door and she followed her to
her father's room. But, alas, the prepared floor opened
under her and she fell staight into a vat of boiling water.
Calmly, Ay took her dead sister's garments and, thus
attired, went to the palace.

Following her mother's sound advice, the saga-
cious girl pretended that she was ill and must keep to
her own room. The king came to see her, but only in
the semi-darkness, so he did not detect the deception.
Besides, Ay had put a magic pommade on her lips and
thus enchanted the king. But the latter was a man of
strong will and not easily overpowered by any spell,
Soon he became sad and distrait.

Uay, drowned in the boiling water, took the form
of a parrot in her next reincarnation. She flew into the
palace grounds and perched near the window of the
king's bedroom. The sacred trees had now withered,
The parrot kept singing this refrain:
"Sire, your trees are dying,
Soon you will be crying.
The fates have snapped the thread.
You'll find your true love dead."

The king paid no attention at first, but as the
bird sang on, he realised the truth and asked the bird to
tell him the whole story. Then he ordered a golden cage
to be made for the parrot and put it in his bedroom.
Before he could do anything more, however, an urgent
royal duty called him up country, a white elephant was

seen up north and he had to go and hunt this animal of good omen. But it grieved him to leave the bird alone in his palace.

The false queen suspected the bird's influence over the king, now that the king was absent, she gave the bird to the cook. The latter plucked the bird, which pretended to be dead. The cook left it and went into the garden to pick some vegetables. In the meantime, with a supreme effort, the bird forced itself into a mouse hole. When the cook came back into the kitchen and found no bird, she was so frightened that she did not dare tell the truth to her queen. She just bought another parrot and prepared everything just as had been ordered for the royal dinner. The queen was very pleased with the cook and gave her a scarf as a reward.

The mouse was full of compassion for the unfortunate bird. He nursed the bird and took care of her until she was well enought to seek another and safer place. Then he took her to the other opening that he had made and which led to the forest, and bade her safe journey.

All by herself and deprived of wings, weak and forlorn, the parrot made her way slowly through strange places. She was exposed to many and varied dangers. Once a serpent was on the point of eating her, but fortunately, the serpent itself was attacked by a big bird and thus she was saved. Her strength was almost exhausted, when she came upon an anchorite. He took pity upon her and put her near the fire, the sacred object of his meditation. Suddenly the bird vanished and a beautiful young maiden rose from the flames: it was Uay, to whom the gods had granted a new life. Full of gratitude, Uay prostrated herself at the feet of the holy man, asking permission to serve him till the end of her life. But the old sage whose life was dedicated to prayer and solitude, thought that it would be wiser to create another human being to keep her company. So he drew a picture of a small boy five years of age and gave it the breath of life, this boy was named Lop.

Uay was very happy now. Restored to human life again, she now spent her time with Lop gathering fruits for the hermit. Many a time, she thought of her royal consort, especially when the child asked about his father and his kinsfolk. Then she would explain to the boy. "Lop, you are my child, and I am the child of this holy man. Your father is a king." But the lad wanted to know more about his royal father. Curious, the boy said: "Mother, let me go to the palace".

"My child," she replied, "would you know how to take care of yourself?. Many dangers lie ahead of you". "The gods will protect me, Mother; you always say that the gods look after their creatures," insisted the boy. "Let me go to see my father, Mother. All the good that you have done shall be like a shield for my protection.

I do want to see the trees with leaves of gold and silver, if they are still there, and I do want to see my father."

Lop's entreaties and insistance finally persuaded Uay to let him go to the city. She put around his neck a garland of flowers on which she inscribed the story of the white elephant hunt, the usurper's crime, the flight of the wingless bird, the resurrection and the creation of the boy.

Lop went to the city; he enjoyed himself tremendously, not noticing that people stared at him, wondering: "Whose child is this? What a queer chain he is wearing!" and so forth.

Soon this news reached the king and Lop was brought into his royal presence. The monarch asked the boy to tell about his errand, and the boy said he wanted to see the miraculous trees. Great was the king's surprise, but greater still when he saw the garland round the boy's neck. The king could see the interpretation on the garland. He asked the boy questions, and the boy did not disappoint him, for young though he was, he was also very intelligent, and soon the king knew of Uay's existence; and he went to her in the forest.

When the holy man saw the king, he knew that both happiness and grief were in store for Uay; for it was written that when she saw her husband again she would lose what she cherished most. Lop would turn into an image again as soon as he was seven years old and that would be in three days' time. The hermit called the girl and told her what the future held for her. He then entreated her to leave the forest; her duty was to follow her royal husband.

Thus Uay left the hermit and came into the city. The people celebrated the queen's happy return for seven days and seven nights. The half-sister and her cook were brought to trial and they confessed their crimes. They were not killed, but put into prison.

Uay had suffered a great deal, but her meditations had made her more compassionate and less vindictive. She realised that a bad action must not be answered by another bad one. Evil must be overcome by good. It is better to stop the circle of reincarnation. After much pleading, she obtained a pardon for the two guilty women. But it was too late for her half-sister, Ay poisoned herself while she was in prison.

Uay's father had been cruel to his own flesh and blood and the step-mother had killed Uay for the sake of Ay. The King ordered that Ay's body be sent to Sethi in a jar. The parents were very proud of their daughter being a queen. They boasted so much about her. Now, when they received a present from the palace, they believed that the queen, their daughter, had provided meat for her family. But soon they realised with terror that their crimes were discovered, and they fled into the deep forest,

Now there came at this time a wise man to the kingdom of Thao Phrommathat. The king received the holy man royally. He asked him to explain to them the cause of Uay's misfortunes, for Uay had done no wrong to her fellow creatures. This was what he told them:

"In one of her previous lives Kanitha, Uay's mother, had separated a chicken from its mother; she took the hen to the gods and gave the chicken to her own child to play with. But the chicken cried and ran after its mother and fell into a pot of boiling water. Thus Uay was separated from her mother and killed in the same way."

"But," asked the king, "when she became a bird and was on the point of being killed, why was she saved?"

"In one of her previous lives, she was a vulture, Ay was a chicken. The bird of prey was taking the chicken up to its eyes, but she let it go by accident, and that is why Uay was saved."

"Most noble father," asked the king, "why did Sethi kill his first wife?"

"Sethi once took the form of a talkative parrot and was cherished by its owner. In that same reincarnation, Kanitha took the form of a cat, living in the same house as the parrot. The cat was jealous of the parrot and, when the owner was absent, she killed the bird. That was why he hated her and let her drown."

"Every act has its consequence and repeats itself reciprocally until one a party realises the essence of life and ceases to return evil for evil. Then little by little we eliminate our own reincarnations and come to that blissful joy of pure serenity which saves us from this dreary and vicious world."

The King and Uay forgave Sethi and his wife Kanithi. They asked the culprits to leave their hiding place and to come and live at court.

The King and Uay spent the rest of their lives virtuously and lived together in perfect harmony till the end of their long and peaceful lives.

THE EYES
OF THE
TWELVE QUEENS

Once upon a time, there was a rich man named Nôn,[1] who was blessed with every thing he wanted, except children.

One day, he said to himself: "These bananas are the first fruits of the season. I'll take them to the temple and offer them to the priests: The gods will bless me and grant my wish!"

He took the twelve beautiful bananas and did as he planned.

The next year, at the same season a daughter was born to him, and thereafter each year, at the same time, was born another daughter, then another, until his daughters were twelve in number.

As time went on, Nôn found himself with a great deal of trouble. There was so much to do that the servants all left him. And his expenses for the twelve daughters were so great that soon he was bankrupt. Furious, he took the twelve unfortunate girls into the forest and left them there to die.

These twelve daughters wandered around the forest. The gods took pity upon them and led them into the forest of a kind old ogress named Sontha-marn.[2] This ancient ogress changed her form into

---

1. Nandana.   2. Sandha mara.

that of a human being and then came to meet the
twelve girls and took them to her home and cared
for them.

Years passed by, and they all lived very happily
until one day, the first sister came running from the
garden and said to the other sisters.

"Oh! listen my sisters, I'm very much afraid
that our benefactress is not a human being!"

Second Sister   — Impossible!

Fourth Sister   — Unbelievable!

Fifth Sister   — Please, do not try to kid us this way.

Eleventh Sister   — If she were an ogress, why has not
                    she eaten us up.

First Sister   — Well, come and look for yourself.

They went into the garden and found, to their
horror, heaps of human bones hidden in a remote
corner. After that, they watched closely the comportment
of their hostess and realised the whole truth. They
were very grateful to Sonthamarn, but doubts began
to creep into their young minds. And one day, loosing
their heads, they all fled away from their benefactress.

Sonthamarn found their absence unbearable
and went after them. Terrified, the twelve sisters hid
themselves near the wild elephants'den and asked the
elephants not to tell to the ogress. The etephants kept
their promise and when inquired by Sonthamarn,
they told her to go just the opposite direction. The
twelve girls continued their way and each time the
ogress was close to them, they asked the bears, the
tigers, the horses, the cows etc. to shelter their hiding
place and mislead the follower. Tired and broken hearted

the kind Sonthamarn went back to her palace to live in solitude, grudging at her own kind - heartedness and vowing vengeance to the twelve ungrateful human beings.

The twelve sisters fled onward and onward until they came to the outskirt of a country named Kootara Nakorn.[1] It happened that Rothasit,[2] the king of Kootara Nakorn sent his hunch-back maid, Nang Khom (=Dame Hunch-back), to fetch water for his bath. This ugly girl came to the large lake at the outskirt of the city, where there was a big bunyan tree. There she rested for a while. Then as she bent herself to take the water, she saw the beautiful reflexion in the clear water, which she thought to be herself and she exclaimed:

"May the boons of the gods help me! What! I am thus beautiful and I am still the lowest slave? I can do something better than such common irksome work as fetching the water...... any poor slave can do that!........"

Furious at being so much abused Nang Khom broke the jar and went to explain her behaviour to the King.

The idea was so grotesque that it made the king laugh. He did not punish her, but gave her a silver bucket to fetch water with. The same incident happened again and the king, to amuse himself, gave her a bucket made of leather and ordered her to do her usual duty.

---

1. Gutara Nagara.   2. Radha Siddhi.

The slave girl saw the beautiful reflexion again and again she was outraged at the lowest duty bestowed upon her. She tried to destroy the leather, but in vain. But as she was struggling with this instrument, she heard somebody laughing above her. Looking up she saw a group of beautiful goddesses on the banyan. The sight filled her with awe and she fled away to report to the King.

Rothasit was very much amused at Nang Khom's tale of goddesses. However, he commanded his prime minister to bring to his royal presence the goddesses in question........They were no other than the twelve daughters of Nôn.

Great was the compassion of King Rothasit, when he learned about their misforture. He allowed them to stay in his palace and in due time asked them to be his queen.s The people were very pleased to have so many beautiful queens in their country, they celebrated the royal wedding for twelve days and twelve nights. News reached other cities and they travelled to see them and praised about their beauty. Kootara Nakorn soon prospered and they all lived very happily.

One day as the monarch came back from the hunt, he saw a girl of wonderous beauty standing by the lake under the bunyan tree. He fell in love with her at the very instant: for she was no other than the ogress Sonthamarn, who took the form of a girl to lure the king. It was her time now to pay back the ingratitude of the twelve beautiful human beings.

Since the arrival of Sonthamarn, Nôn's twelve daughters had no peace. None of their endeavour to please the king seemed to be fruitful. And soon they were banished from the royal presence and confined to their inner court.

One day Sonthamarn pretended to be gravely ill. The court physicians were powerless before such a strange illness. Days passed by and the King's anxiety knew no bound. One day seeing Sonthamarn's great suffering, he said:

"I will give half of my kingdom to one who can cure my queen!"

"— My most noble King" said Sonthamarn, the cure of my illness will not cost you that much, but 1 prefer rather to die than ask it of you........

The loving husband pressed her to tell him her desire, promising to grant her all her wishes beforehand.

"My Lord, the medicine which will restore me to my health need the eyes of twelve beautiful human beings to mix with."

........The king was taken aback, but as he had promised to grant her what she wanted, he complied to her wishes.

Besides herself with joy, the ogress could hardly wait to punish former protegees. As soon as they were taken to her presence she jomped out of her bed and took the eyes out of the wretched queens. The youngest sister who used to be her pet was left one eye, fortunately. Sonthamarn then sent these twenty three human eyes to her daughter Kang-Ree, who was ruling over a city name Kocha Pura Nakorn. [1] As for the blind queens, she caused them to be put into a tunnel, under a far-off mountain, and ordered that the opening be sealed.

When these girls were driven away from the court, they were all pregnant. In spite of their misery, they manage to be alive and in due time, one by one, they gave birth to children which they ate. The twelfth sister would not eat her share, she roasted the meal, of her sisters' children and hid away. When her child was born, she took him out of their reach. In stead of killing the child, she gave them the human flesh she had preserved and thus paid her share to the community.

With much pain and unimaginable hardship, the youngest queen managed to keep her boy alive. Now that he grew to be able to take care of himself, the mother broke the news to her elder sisters. They could not grudge at this mother: for the boy could sneak out of the tunnel and brought them some food and thus their lives became bearable.

The fatherless boy was called Rothasen,[2] in remembrance of his royal father "Rothasit". Now that

---

1. *Gaja pura Nagara.*   2. *Radha sena.*

he advanced in years, he wandered further and further from the forest. He was strong and healthy and could get even with the children at the outskirt of the forest. Soon, he became the leader. He liked betting and when he won, he always asked for twelve parcels of food. He had a clever fighting cock, which always won and brought him food to take back to his twelve mothers........

Many years passed away, and Rothasen grew to be a stalwart young man. He learnt the truth about his mother and aunts and vowed to the gods he would save them as soon as possible. Hearing that the King Rothasit liked playing "SKA"[1] ( ) Rothasen Learnt and tried to play the game to perfection. The news of his championship reached the king as intended and the Monarch ordered the young man into his presence.

· Now, Rothasen played SKA with the king every day and own the game three days successively. Sonthamarn was anxious at the king's interest in this handsome young stranger, and she always kept him in her sight. At each defeat, the king had to pay twelve parcels of food and could get no explanation from his opponent.

But by keen observation and cleverly turned conversation, the king learnt that the young man is no other than his own son. The realisation brought such happiness upon Rothasit's expression that Sontha-marn became quite worried.

---

1. Backgammon

Subtlely, she left the game-hall, got into her bed and pretended to be suddenly taken ill in order to divert the King's attention from the newly found son.

King Rothasit was alarmed at this grave illness; Sonthamarn suggested that he should send this daring young man to fetch some ingredients for her medicine which are called: "Mamuang roo haw," (the mango that can yawn), "Manao roo ho" (the lime that can shout) which can be found in the Kocha Pura Nakorn (her daughter's city)

To young Rothasen, the King gave Sonthamarn's letter to be delivered urgently to the ruler of Kocha Pura Nakorn. In this letter, the ogress told her daughter in the style of the sorceress thus:—

> This valiant young man
> is called Rothasen,
> and is my worst enemy.
>
> If he comes to you in day time,
> kill him in day time.
> If he comes to you in night time,
> kill him in night time.

Rothasen tied the message to the harnest and set out of his voyage. He travelled for many days, believing that the medicine was really needed. One day he passed by an anchorite's hut, he was so tired that he felt asleep in front of the hut, under a big tree.

The wise old man by his wisdom, knew about the coded message. He took pity of this innocent youth, and, using the same style, he wrote down a new message:

My dear daughter Kang Ree,
I send thee a royal gift.
This valiant young man
is named Rothasen,
son of King Rothasit.
If he comes to thee in day time,
welcome him well in day time.
If he comes to thee in night time,
welcome him in night time.
Take him as thy dear husband.

The valiant young prince came to Kocha Pura Nakorn and things came to pass as was written in the massage.

Though Kang Ree proved to be an enchanting wife, she could not arrive to absorb him entirely. To her, he seemed absent-minded, and she tried her utmost to divert him. Little by little he tried to figure out the truth. Thus he learnt that Sonthamarn was the mother of his wife, as he had always suspected. The news filled him with joy. Still there was something more to learn, but hopes began to dawn in his filial heart: he can restore the sight to his mothers and help them out of their misery.

But days, weeks, months, passed by without further result and he grew more restless. His stay must not exceed the seventh month or else he would be totally under the spell of his witch-wife. One day, with apparent indifference, Rothasen asked his wife to visit her secret garden. Kang Ree was rather reluctant.

"My darling, said the young prince, let us go up there and drink to our half a year's married life."

To this sentimental plea, Kang Ree found no pretext to refuse and they went to the secret spring garden. The Prince poured Kang Ree glasses and glasses of strong alcoholic drinks, while he himself pretended to do the same and even was apparently drunk (still now in the monkey show, the most popular theme is this scene where the verses run:

> Two tumblers, three tumblers
> He gave her
> And the drunken dame
> Fell fast asleep).

He had nonchalantly asked her about the different plants and herbs in the garden. Rothasen also learnt where was the parcel containing the eyes........ When the sorceress fell fast asleep, he then took the parcel containing the eyes and other parcels containing magic weapons and fled away from Kocha Pura Nakorn.

Great was the deception of the loving Kang Ree when she woke up and found that her royal consort was gone. She hurriedly went after him and by her witchery she went so fast that she almost reach him. But Rothasen threw down a parcel of magic powder........There arose a big fire behind him, separating him thus from his wife.

Kang Ree then sat down on the ground and performed the ceremony to stop this unearthly flame. Soon, the way was clear and she followed her husband onward.

Another parcel of magic powder was thrown. There was a tremenduss chain ot mountains, barring Kang Ree's pursuit. She lost time in performing another ceremony. When she came close to him, she begged him to let her go with him, promising to quit her witchery and vowed fidelity to him forever. But Rothasen took no heed to her prayer.

Another pareel was thrown and an enormous dense forest separated them. Kang Ree was so furious that, summoning all her courage and concentration she forced herself through more quickly than before. She then threatened him, invoking upon him all the curse of the witch's family, invoquing all the patrons of the sorcerers. But nothing could stop the valiant Prince. He threw down another parcel and there stretched in front of Kang Ree, an enormous desert.

Outraged at her own powerlessness, Kang Ree spent a long time to overcome the magic desert. Soon it disappeared, but only to be changed into a cyclone. The poor sorceress summoned her last magic knowledge and with the utmost effort, caused the strong tempest to subside. She then called out to her departing husband: she would follow him no longer, nay, she could do nothing more. She was resigned to her fate, but before she breathed her last, let her see his handsome face for the last time. And before they parted for ever, let her give him her knowledge, as a token of her sincere love for him. But the Prince turned a deaf ear and throwing another parcel on the ground, caused a wide river with a strong current to keep the witch's daughter from following him and went steadily onward.

No one could imagine the sorrow and the desperation of this young wife. She rebelled against the gods for being born a witch, for having been given the heart and the feeling of a human being. She hated her own witchcraft, her family, her own mother. She blamed Fate for having led this handsome husband to her. Why this punishment befell on her? She had done him no harm no wrong! Millions of sentiments arose in her young loving heart and it was more than she could stand. Better quit this ugly world. She tried to think of her good actions in her life, so that she might become a real human beingin her next reincarnation. Then she stopped her own breathing and died looking at her fugitive husband.

Rothasen went on for seven days and seven nights, afraid to stop. He arrived at last at the entrance to the tunnel. He restored the eyes to his mother and aunts, healed them with the magic medicine he brought and gave them the elixir of health. While he was thus trying to fulfill his vow, Kang Ree's soul came to tell woeful tales to her mother. Sonthamarn was so surprised, so shocked that she lost all her witch carft, This revelation was such a heavy blow that her old heart could not stand it and it broke into twelve pieces.

At that moment the tunnel suddenly opened. The twelve unfortunate queens regained not only their sight, but also their health and beauty. Now that the sorceress' spell was over, the King realised the truth. He invites the queens to come back to his palace and gave them all the wealth and happiness he could afford, to compensate the long unjust sufferings they had to endure And thus ended the misfortune of the twelve Queens and they lived very happily ever afterwards, seeing the children of their children until the fourth generation.

THE

GOLDEN FLOWER

Phikool Thong[1] was a princess, and very lovely. She was bathing in a beautiful river with some of her ladies-in-waiting.

Phikool Thong: "Oh, the water is so nice and cool today. It's wonderful, I don't want to go home yet."

First Lady-in-waiting: "But it is getting late, Princess; see, the sun is high in the sky; it must be nearly time for the priests' lunch."[2]

Second Lady-in-waiting: "Please don't speak about going home yet!"

Third Lady-in-waiting: "We've never enjoyed ourselves so much."

First Lady-in-waiting: "I agree with you, my friends, but we are all afraid of the king's displeasure."

---

1. Phikool is a small, sweet-smelling, yellow flower, not much larger than a forget-me-not. Thong means gold..... Phikool Thong is a girl's name and the name of the heroine of this story.

2. 11 o'clock a.m. is the time for the priests' last meal of the day. According to the Buddhist commandments, priests cannot take any solid form of nutriment from 12 noon till 6 a.m. the next day. We usually offer the meal to them at 11 a.m., and this time is called Pali. Etymologically, it is a word of Sanskrit origin meaning "time"

Phikool Thong: "You're right. Let us get out of the water, but let us walk home by the path near the temple. The *Phutsa* tree must be laden with ripe fruit now."

But before they got out of the water, they saw the carcase of a dog, with a vulture perched on it voraciously devouring his carrion meal.

Phikool Thong: "Ugh, that vile bird!"

First Lady-in-waiting: "He likes filth!"

Second Lady-in-waiting: "That's why he smells like a corpse!"

Third Lady-in-waiting: "Don't you know that he is a bird of ill omen? Wherever he alights, something disastrous always happens; ruin, destruction, or death."

Phikool Thong: "Come, let us get away from here. The smell is terrible. This bird is disgusting. May I never see him again as long as I live."

So saying, the princess ran away with her companions to the temple yard. The sight and the smell had made them all feel sick.

Now, the bird was none other than King Vulture himself. And, of course, he was not accustomed to such treatment. He grew very angry and vowed vengeance against the beautiful princess and her party.

Phikool Thong was the daughter of the famous King Sanuraj[1] and was widely known for her great beauty and charm. Her hair had a wonderful perfume, and every time she spoke, golden flowers used to fall from her lips. That is why they called her *Phikool Thong*.

King Vulture, to carry out his plan of revenge, took the form of a handsome young man. He went to live with a poor old couple in Sanuraj's kingdom, then asked his foster parents upon whom he bestowed many riches to approach the king on his behalf and beg for the princess' hand in marriage.

The king was annoyed at the presumption of this unknown young man; but he did not want to risk the criticism of his subjects by killing or punishing this seemingly inoffensive young man. Instead, he set him what appeared to be an impossible task; he was to build a bridge of gold and a birdge of silver from his hut to the king's palace, by the following morning. If he failed, he and his descendants were to be punished for seven generations. But the full task was accomplished by the bird's magic power, and thus King Sanuraj had to give his daughter to King Vulture in human form.

No one could imagine Phikool Thong's misery. Every time the young man approached her, she felt overcome by the smell of the vulture. The young husband was furious, but he prudently restrained his anger.

1. *Sonuraja*

He went to see his father-in-law, and asked the latter to grant him permission to take Phikool Thong to his home. Sanuraj did not wish to let his beloved daughter go, but he could not very well refuse his permission to such a normal request. So, for the first time in Phikool Thong's life, she had to leave her dear father, and the bare thought filled her with terror.

The young husband took her down to his ship, where all the crew worked in silence. They travelled all day, and by the late afternoon, the ship was drifting alone on the ocean. There was nothing in sight but the vast expanse of sea and sky. Suddenly the young man and his crew disappeared, leaving Phikool Thong wandering alone about the ship. Terrified, she wondered what would happen to her next. Then a huge black cloud appeared over the ship. It proved to be a tremendous swarm of vultures headed by King Vulture who had reverted to his natural form. Though she could not know that, this was really her husband. She was so astounded that she stood on the deck, not knowing what to do. Then softly, out of the stillness, she heard a voice: "My child, my child, you are in danger, but do as I say and all will be well. I will help you. But, first, do not stand there in the open, hide yourself."

Terrified, the young girl turned around. At first, she saw nothing but the ship's main mast. Then all of a sudden she noticed a large hole in the great spar and, frenzied with fear, she rushed over and crawled into it. As she settled down inside the mast, the opening closed behind her. Outside, she heard great confusion and shrieking, with the rustle of wings. After a while, this was followed by dead silence......... She must have fallen asleep, for when she opened her eyes again, she saw a beautiful girl with a lovely golden complexion and long black hair that fell in luxuriant folds over her smooth, wellrounded shoulders. She was dressed all in red, in a *Phasin* and *Sabai*[1]

"Dear Princess," said the beautiful stranger in her soft, clear voice, "calm your fear. You are safe now with me. I am the goddess of this ship and I shall watch over you and help you."

She then told the whole story of her misfortunes to Phikool Thong, who was terrified anew at the apparent magic power of her vulture husband. She beseeched the goddess to stay with her always and protect her. The goddess then assured her that soon a real prince would come and rescue her from her peril and that she would at last be freed from the vulture's vengeance.

Phikool Thong was afraid to leave her hiding place, for all her own followers had been killed and

---

1. Phasin, the traditional Siamese skirt, consists of a piece of cloth (about 1 m. by 2.30 m.) wrapped around the waist and falling to the ankles. It is usually worn with a silver or a gold belt. Sabai is the upper garment, favoured by Siamese women, and consisting of a piece of cloth about 20 cm. by 1.50 m. One end is draped over to the left of the neck, leaving the right shoulder bare.

their bones lay heaped on the deck. Besides, King Vulture kept coming back again and again to make sure that the disdainful princess had not survived the destruction. Moreover, the goddess of the ship had told her to stay in her sanctuary. Then one day the goddess told her to go and swim beside the ship.

While Phikool Thong was bathing; she ran her fingers through her hair and one of her hairs came out in her hand. She put it in a small golden locket, together with a message telling the position of the ship. This in turn she sealed tight in a casket and set afloat on the sea. As it was being carried away by the current, the Princess murmured this prayer: "Most Noble Mother of the Sea, if I am to survive this ordeal, pray bring this token of mine to my rescuer."

The Goddess of the Sea took pity on the forlorn Princess. It so happened that King Phichai[1] who was enjoying the evening breeze on the deck of his ship, saw the casket of Phikool Thong floating by; he caused it to be brought into his royal presence. When he learned of the princess' plight, he set sail at once for the indicated place.

But one night, on the way, his ship had to pass by the island of the notorious ogress, known as Kakhao.[2] When Kakhao saw the handsome king sleeping on the deck of his ship, she caused the vessel to be diverted from its course and stopped at her island. By her magic skill, she cast a spell over

---

1. Vijaya   2. White crow

the sailors and courtiers and sent them into a deep sleep,
But the king she took into her inner court, awoke him
and tried by all her wiles and magic incantations to bind
him to her for ever, but to no avail. He pretended to
fall a willing victim to her charms, but when she fell
asleep, he escaped from her clutches and betook himself
back to his own ship. He did not wake his crew up,
but by himself hoisted sail and glided off into the misty
night.

The dawning light of a new day aroused them
and they found themselves not far away from Phikool
Thong's deserted ship. At that very moment King
Vulture again made his appearance over the refuge of
his human bride. But it proved to be his last, for
the king, seeing the vulture hovering overhead, killed
him. Phichai then took Kink Sanuraj's daughter back
to his kingdom and married her amid great pomp and
ceremony.

Phikool Thong led a very happy and peaceful
life with her royal consort and begat two sons, whom
she named Luk and Yom. One day, Phikool Thong
went out with her sons to gather some lotus flowers in
the lake near the forest. The ogress Kakhao, who had
vowed vengeance upon her, lay in wait in the lake and
took the form of a beautiful lotus. When Phikool Thong
stretched out her hand to pluck the flower, the ogress
seized her hand and drew her into the water, changing
her into a gibbon. The ogress herself then took the form

of Phikool Thong and was rescued by the courtiers, thus returning triumphantly to the king's palace.

The king, who was madly in love with Phikool Thong, was completely deceived by this impostor and could not understand why his two sons refused to come to their mother. The children insisted that their real mother was the gibbon that they had seen by the lake. "Please, my Lord", said the supposed mother, "send my sons to their gibbon, since they do not want their own mother any more."

Luk and Yom went out of their father's home and came to see their mother, though she was in the form of a gibbon. Their mother advised them to pick up the golden flowers which had fallen from her mouth and to sell them in the market. The boys did as their mother said, and it so happened that King Sanuraj, the father of Phikool Thong, heard about these strange flowers being sold, so he ordered his servants to bring him some. When the flowers were brought to him, he recognised at once the magic blossoms which came from his own daughter's mouth. Fearful for the safety of his daughter, Sanuraj sent a message of King Phichai, telling the story of Phikool Thong inquiring about her, and urging Phichai to go and see the gibbon without delay.

Phichai hid himself in a bush and sent his sons to ask their mother what to do. The gibbon told them that she must see King Phichai immediately. When he was sure of her identity he went to ask her forgiveness.

She told him that he must hasten lest the golden hair on her forehead grew long, because then she would not be able to bear the company of humans, but would have to go and hide deep in the forest. She told him to kill the false Phikool Thong and to bring her blood in order that she, the true wife, might bathe herself in it.

Phichai followed her instructions, killed the false wife, and brought her blood to Phikool Thong who, on bathing in it, was transformed again into her real self, the lovely queen whose hair had an unforgettable fragrance and from whose lips dropped golden blossoms whenever she spoke.

Many years passed, during which time King Pichai and Queen Phikool Thong were immensely happy, both in their love for each other and in their deep delight at seeing their small sons grow into stalwart, handsome young men.

One day Phikool Thong missed her former home so much that she begged her husband to take her and her sons to her father's home, so that the grandparents could see and admire the two handsome boys. So they set sail for the land of King Sanuraj, but unfortunately, they had to pass again by the island of the wicked sorceress, Kakhao, whose sister Kasurat had vowed vengeance upon them. As they passed the island, Kasurat caused a fearful tempest to arise, which wrecked the ship.

Phikool Thong, in a state of unconsciousness, was washed ashore by a huge wave. When she recovered, she found herself on a lonely beach. Terrified and forlorn, because of the loss of her husband and children, she sat sobbing a long time. Then suddenly she remembered her magic ring. She took it from her finger and said this prayer: "O, most sacred Gods who rule the world, if it is my fate to live to see my husband and children again, let this ring float on the surface of the water."

She then threw her ring into the sea. Again the Goddess of the Sea took pity on her. She caused the ring to float upon the surface of the water. Seeing this miracle, Phikool Thong regained her courage and, cutting a piece out of her *sabai,* she wrote a message on it, telling in which direction she planned to go. She tied it to a stick of wood which she planted firmly in the ground.

As she was journeying eastward, she was terrified out of her senses to meet a huge and hideous giant. This was none other than Viroonchak,[1] the owner of the island. He forced her to follow him to his palace. His prayers, his entreaties, his threats—nothing could turn Phikool Thong from her fidelity to her husband. Enraged, Viroonchak snatched his sword to kill her, but even as he dealt the blow, the sword itself refused to strike so virtuous a woman. Instead of striking her breast, it jabbed into the floor, breaking into two pieces. Awed by such a miraculous incident, Viroonchak

1. Viruncakra

dared no more to try to kill her, but still feeling bitter and resentful, he banished her to the kitchen to do the most menial work of a scullery maid.

While all this was happening to Phikool Thong, let us see what happened to Phichai and his sons. A few hours after the departure of Phikool Thong from the beach, where she had left her *sabai* flag, the king and his sons were washed ashore at the same place. They found the message and set out in search.

In their wanderings they came to the dwelling of a hermit who had the gift of prophecy. He advised them to stay with him until the period of ill-fortune was over. They followed his kind advice and learnt a great deal about magic and all kinds of knowledge.

One day the sage told them that the time was ripe for them to go and find Phikool Thong. They bade farewell to the hermit and expressed their gratitude for his hospitality, then they left him, They journeyed for several days and finally came to the palace of Viroonchak. There, in the garden, they saw the giant's daughter who fell in love with King Phichai. The latter and his sons put on magic rings which had power to turn them into any form they chose. They took the forms of minor birds, and flew into the Princess Aroon Vadi's palace. There, they resumed the form of human beings and for a time lived happily in her court.

This clandestine life could not go on without the knowledge of the courtiers, who, of course, duly reported to the king. Viroonchak hastened to the palace of his daughter, and seeing proof of this rumour, he challenged King Phichai to fight. In the course of the fight, the giant was killed, and thus King Phichai became the ruler of the giant's kingdom.

No one could imagine the grief and sorrow of the faithful Phikool Thong, who was forced to be one of the lowliest of slaves of her own husband and his new wife. But she waited patiently for an opportunity to reveal her true identity.

One day, when the cook was not looking, she hid one of her beautiful golden flowers in the food, which was to be served to the king. When Phichai found this token, he ordered her to be brought into his royal presence. There was great joy because of the reunion of husband and wife and sons, and the whole kingdom celebrated for seven days and seven nights.

Then, according to custom, the king called Aroon Vadi to kneel and pay homage to his first wife. But the young princess refused, saying that she would not prostrate herself to a woman who had been unfaithful to her husband; she accused Phikool Thong of being her late father's concubine.

Outraged, Phikool Thong demanded to be given trial by fire, which request the king granted her. In this trial, Indra, the God of Gods, proved the purity

of this faithful queen by letting a cool breeze to blow
upon her tiny feet so that the flames would cause her
no harm whatever. He also caused a rain of celestial
flowers to fall around her, as further testimony to
her purity. Great was the joy of those who witnessed
this miracle, and loudly they sang the praises of Phikool
Thong and honoured her in the most noble fashion.

But greater was the shame and vexation of the
heartless Aroon Vadi. She could not stand having the
first wife in her way. She went to her sorceress mother
and, by their witchery, they made one of their slaves to
take the form of Phikool Thong, whilst they cast the
real queen into a dungeon. The king, completely deceived, was highly pleased with the false Phikool Thong,
who in turn used all her guile and power of enchantment.

The king and the two princes undertook the
long-awaited voyage to the kingdom of Sanuraj. The
false Phikool Thong and Aroon Vadi accompanied them.
King Sanuraj and his queen were very pleased to see
their only daughter. As they had not seen her for a long
time, they could not realise what changes had taken
place. They were surprised not to see the golden flowers falling from her mouth and missed the sweet fragrance
of her beautiful hair.

Luk and Yom told their grandparents about their
eventful life and their suspicions against the false Phikool
Thong. That night, both of them had the same dream:
they saw their mother in a dark cell under the palace.
The next day they set forth on a journey.

King Sanuraj summoned his royal son-in-law to his presence. After much persuasion and long discussion King Phichai began to see the whole train of events more clearly. He set out with his army towards the country to which Aroon Vadi's mother had fled, hoping to threaten her into telling the truth about Phikool Thong. He knew that only this last queen of the giants' race possessed such potent witchcraft.

Sanuraj was a wise old king. He summoned the false Phikool Thong to his presence and asked her to prove that she was his own daughter. The sly creature. was so clever, however, that she had an answer for every question: she lost the perfume of her hair while she lived in the company of vultures and the flowers stopped falling from her mouth when they changed her into a gibbon. King Sanuraj and his wife could not bring themselves to harm this strange creature. Then his wife remembered one thing and triumphantly asked: "Now, if you are my daughter, let me see the beauty-spot on your breast."

Alarmed, the girl forgot the magic with which she could have caused the beauty spot to appear. Also she was at a loss in not knowing on which breast the beauty-spot was supposed to be. Seeing no mark on the left breast of the false Phikool Thong and observing all her nervousness, King Sanuraj ordered her to be whipped with a branch of the Mayom tree.[1]

---

1. A tree bearing acid fruits. They use its leaves to sprinkle holy water in the ceremony of purification, and its stems for exorcism,

The girl was changed back into her own form. She begged to be allowed to live, promising to take them to the hiding place of Queen Phikool Thong.

The king immediately despatched his best warriors to bring back his unfortunate daughter. After a long and eventful voyage, they reached the palace where Phikool Thong was confined. Because of her faithfulness to her husband, the Gods had mercy on her. They had kept her from harm and now led her safely back to her father again.

The fame of her beauty and charm, the strange story of her adventures, travelled far and wide and brought to her court kings and warriors from other powerful nations.

The family was at last reunited and they all lived together thereafter. The Gods willed that no further harm should ever befall the pure and virtuous Phikool Thong, the Golden Flower.

AT THE COUNTRY

OF THE

BIRD-WOMEN

Once upon a time there lived a mighty King called Athityawong.[1] His wife bore that sonorous name of Chanthathevi.[2] They had a handsome son named Suthon,[3] which means good arrow, because of his exceptional skill in archery. His fame travelled far and wide and the neighbouring countries lived in awe of the "Panchala[4] Nakorn".

There was a large lake to the east of this country. In this lake lived a wise old Naga, named Phrya Nak Chompoo Chit.[5] People brought him food, flowers and aromatic sticks as their mark of respects towards him. For this sacred Naga was a sage and by his prayers and long meditations, he had the power of conferring blessing and he gave his benedictions on fruit-trees, cattle and the crops of those people who came to worship him and thus Panchara Nakorn became renowned for its prosperity.

At the same period, there existed to the west of Panchala, another country called Maha-Panchala. It happened that a great famine ravaged the land and as there was no remedy for it, people emigrated slowly to the neighbouring and fertile countries. Seeing the

---

1. Aditaya - Vamsa   2. Candara Devi   3. Sudhana
4. Pancala Nagara   5. Jambhu Citra

population so much decreased in number King Nantharai[1] ordered his prime minister to his presence and said:--

"My dear counsellor, what causes my people to desert me in this manner?"

-- Sire, the cause lies beyond our power -- it is because of the sacred Naga.

-- Please explain yourself more fully.

And the counsellor related to his monarch all about that prosperous country of King Athitayawong

Nantharat   -- Well, let us get rid of this Naga.

Counsellor -- My Lord, that is beyond human power.

Nantharat   -- Come, my dear counsellor, with wise learning, human beings can conquer the world, let alone a mere brute.

Counsellor -- Sir, give me time.

Nantharat   -- Let us make haste and find out the right man for the job.

So the counsellor sent heralds all over the country, beating gongs and announcing the monarch's wish to summon a general meeting of all learned "Pram'[2] in the country.

Soon more than five hundred Brahmins presented themselves before the king. Those Brahmins picked out the most gifted one among them as their spokes-man and the King said unto him:

I. Nanda Raja   2. Brahmins

" Most honourable Brahmin we want to have that famous Naga from the lake on the east of Panchala Nakorn ".

Brahmin   — What will happen if I chance to kill him?

Nantharat   — Bring him to me, dead or alive, and half of my kingdom is yours, upon my word!

And the Brahmin under-took to carry out the king's wish.

"Chomphoo Chit Naga" knew about his impending doom; he felt so restless that he assumed the form of a brahmin, sitting on the bank of the lake. At that moment, a hunter came to the lake to wash the game which he had just killed.

Seeing him the Naga said:

"I come here to see a Brahmin performing a certain ceremony. Where do you come from, and what part have you to do with the ceremony?

Hunter   — I am a hunter and I call myself Boontharik[1] (which means the white lotus). But people contract it into just "Boon". I have no other business than washing the game I've caught.

Naga   — You belong to the place, probably you can tell me how things are getting on here.

Hunter   — Very well indeed! Sir, thanks to our beloved Naga Chomphoo Chit.

---

1. Pundari Ka

Naga	.- (with sorrow in his voice). Do you know that now some-one is planning to kill him?
Hunter	— Heaven forbids! That shall never come to pass. He who does wrong to our Naga, wrongs our country and however powerful he may be, I shall never hesitate to fight him.
Naga	— I know you are a good man, Hunter Boon. I'm going to tell you the truth. I am Chomphoo Chit Naga himself. Now there is a learned Brahmin sent by a rival country to take my life. I beseech you to give me your help.
Hunter	— Oh! Noble Naga! tell me what I have to do and I'll do it with all my might and main!
Naga	— Hide yourself in yonder wood! Pretty soon an artful Brahmin will come. His cloth will be all in white. He'll come this way to rinse his mouth then he'll come and stand over the lake. In his left hand he'll be holding a sheaf of lalang grass. He'll wave his hand towards the lake, chant some "mon"[1] and put some medicine into the lake. As soon as you see the water beginning to get muddy you must shoot at him,

---

[1]. Mantra

taking care, however not to kill him. Then you must rush from your hiding place, and take hold of him by the hair threatening to kill him with your sabre: "Now, cruel Brahmin, take back your bad "mon" else I'll kill you".

Hunter   — But how am I to know that he takes away his bad mantra?

Naga   — Black vapour will rise out of this thick water and the water will be clear again. Then you must cut off his head"

Hunter   — I promise to do as you bid me, Noble Naga.

The Naga then took leave of the hunter and went to his subterranean abode, whilst the hunter hurriedly repaired to the wood near-by to ambush himself there.

In a few moments every thing came to pass as the Naga Chomphoo Chit had predicted. Hunter Boon did as he was bidden. Soon the Naga came upon the surface and invited Hunter Boon to follow him to his underground den, where he entertained him lavishly for seven days, then he accompanied his benefactor to the surface and said:

"Kind Hunter Boon, whenever you need my help, do come to this lake, think hard of the Naga who guards my place and he'll come to fetch you down".

One day, as Hunter Boon went to his customary hunting trip, he wandered further than usual until he came near to the meditating spot of an anchorite by the name of Kadsob. Not far from this place he saw a large beautiful pool surrounded by a magnificent garden, astonished, he prostrated himself before the sage and said:-

    — "Most noble Sir! this place looks as if it is brought about by superhuman agency, being so distant from any human habitation.

Kadsob   — Hunter I've been sitting here for quite a long time, yet I see no-body come to take care of this garden. Once in a while, however, a group of Bird-women, the Kinaree come here and enjoy their bathing.

Hunter   — Where are these Bird-women you speak of? I've heard so much about them, yet I've never come across one.

Kadsob   — Stay here for some time and you shall see for yourself. It is really quite worthwhile.

Hunter   — Is there any way, Sir, for me to catch one of these lovely Bird-Women for my lord the King. Can't you advise me how to compass that end?

Kadsob   — It is not an easy matter, my dear man, unless you have what is known as Naga's noose.

1. Kasapa

Hunter   — What is Naga's noose, Sir, how can I manage to get hold of one.

Kadsob   — Naga's noose belongs to the Naga of Patala, the subterranean world. If you can get one then the snaring of these bird-maidens is simply a matter of child - play.

Having been thus informed, Boon, the Hunter turned his thought to his friend the old Naga Chomphoo Chit. So he made a bee-line to the Naga's pool. He begged the loan of Naga's noose under the pretext of using it as a weapon against Naga's arch-enemy, Garuda. At this apparently reasonable request the old naga could not very well refuse, so the Hunter returned triumphantly to the pool, where he found seven daughters of King Tumarat,[1] after having doffed their wings, tails and other articles of personal adornments, swimming happily, unconscious of the fate that was about to befall one of them. Manora, the youngest and fairest of the Bird-Maidens was the object of Boon the Hunter's attention and he made off with his fair captive to Panchala Nakorn.

When King Athityawong and Queen Chanthathevi found out that Manora was a princess of the blood with all feminine qualifications for future queenship they married her rightaway to their beloved son and heir, Prince Suthon.

---

1. Dumaraja

As fate willed it, one day Prince Suthon, in order to reward one of his favourite Brahmin attendant, promised him the post of Court Counsellor. As this promise happened to reach the ear of the then Court Counsellor, naturally, the man was quite incensed at the prospect of being ousted from his exalted position. From that time onward he cherished in his mind the thought of overthrowing Prince Suthon. Whenever the favourable occasion arrived he went so far as trying to poison the mind of the King that his son was planning to usurp the throne but the King, however, paid him no heed. It happened that soon after this a hostile army gathered at the frontier of the kingdom of Panchala and Prince Suthon was ordered to lead an army to quell it, leaving thereby his newly acquired bird-maiden wife Manora behind.

That very night King Athityawong dreamt a strange dream which frightened him so much that he had to summon the Brahmin Court Counsellor before him and said:

King — My dear Counsellor, last night I dreamt that my intestine became unwound from my bowel and began to spread three times around this island-continent of ours. Suddenly it contracted again and I became awake. Can you tell me what is going to happen?

The Brahmin Counsellor at once seized the long-looked-for opportunity of accusing the Prince, replied:

"May it please Your Majesty, your dream is the portent of a very grave catastrophe about to befall your realm and your royal family."

King — Then is there any way to avoid this approaching misfortune?

Brahmin — In my humble opinion, Sire, Your Majesty ought to propitiate the gods by offering blood sacrifice of bipeds and quadrupeds in accordance with ancient brahminical rites.

King — Now, make your meaning clear.

Brahmin — The offering of sacrifice will bring about untold benefits. Your Majesty and your consort will be very happy and prosperous. Only one thing is lacking however that is a bird-woman as an offering which will be most acceptable to the gods. With Your Majesty's kind permission may I suggest that the one thing needful lies in the person of Your Majesty's daughter-in-law, Manora.

King — She is the most beloved of my dear son, how can I do what will hurt him most?

Brahmin — Your Majesty will have to decide for yourself whether your realm and your subjects mean less to you than a mere daughter-in-law.

The crafty Brahmin Court Counsellor kept on plying on the ear of the King with the idea of offering Manora to placate the gods. In the end the King was prevailed over, and, he weakly yielded to the wicked advice of his Counsellor. In his heart of hearts, however, he felt very sorry for the poor maiden and yet as he was not sure of himself he gave order that the palace door be locked. No one not even the Queen herself, could come into the royal presence.

Queen Chanthathevi became so upset about the whole thing, yet she was quite helpless because the King allowed only the Court Brahmin to see him. All that she could do was to weep which she did very profusely. Manora tried to console her with encouraging words and, before the soldiers were sent out to bring her to the sacrificial ground, she succeeded in persuading the Queen to bring to her, her personal adornments including her wings and tail which were jealously kept away from her. Manora succeeded in donning her wings and tail when the rowdy mob rushed in. Out she flew, bidding farewell to her mother-in-law and headed eastward for the Anchorite's hermitage.

Manora related every thing to the holy man and implored him.

Manora — I crave your kindness to give this piece of kerchief together with this ring to my husband, Prince Suthon, in case he should arrive here in quest of me. Please advise him to give up the attempt because the undertaking is such a perilous one.

Anchorite — I am sure he will follow you all the same. Human nature is so strange.

Manora — In that case, Sir, may I entrust you with some of these talismans and "mon" to protect him from the hazard of the venture, and now, Sir, I must take leave of you.

She then left for her former abode Mount Krailat[1] where a very warm welcome awaited her. She was given a secluded place so that solitude might in time heal her sorrow.

When Prince Suthon was back again at the Capital, after having routed the enemy forces, he learned the sad news of his wife's precipitated departure. He rushed out, leaving every thing behind, with one set purpose, namely, to be joined once more with beauteous Manora. Ultimately he reached the Anchorite's cottage and the holy man gave him all that his wife deposited there, not forgetting her paradoxical wish that he would give up the pursuit. As the Prince was most adamant in his determination, the holy man gave him the protective talismans as well as all necessary incantations in order to enable him to reach the land of the bird-folks.

---

1 Kailasa

. Prince Suthon learned by rote all the "mon" and the use of all talismans and he kept also a pet monkey which he used as taster for all jungle-fruits before he partook of them himself, thereby keeping safe from eating poison fruits and berries. He took a northerly course, trudging through thorny paths through interminable jungles, for seven years seven months and seven days when he reached the abode of a Yak[1] of immense stature breathing brimstone and smoke out of his nostrils and staring with fiery eyes at the Prince. With incantations and talismans he managed to get rid of this ogre, but then another obstacle appeared before him. A river of vitriol barred his way. With some of the drugs given him by the Anchorite smeared on both feet he managed to step on to the back of a huge boa-constrictor which enabled him to cross the caustic stream into the sharp-pointed cane-brakes; then he came across a solitary, gigantic tree which he climbed up and rested himself in the bole of that tree. Soon birds of immense size began to come to roost on that tree and the Prince, with his newly acquired knowledge of the languages of beasts and birds as taught him by the hermit, managed to eaves drop the following dialogue of two chatty birds:

1st bird   — Where shall we seek for our food tomorrow, dear ?

2nd bird   — Let's go to Mount Krailat.

---

1. Yaksa

Tomorrow King Tumarat will perform a ceremony of purification for his daughter recently arrived back from the human regions. She will then be completely cleansed of all offending scent contracted through her stay with human beings.

1st bird : Very well, then, we shall have quite enough of the offerings to satisfy our appetite.

Prince Suthon was very pleased and as soon as he found them in sound slumber, he managed to get himself tied to the feather of one of the birds which, as morning came, took him unconsciously right to the edge of a lotus pond in King Tumarat's mountain domain. He hid himself in the nearby bush awaiting for the development of the events. Soon several bird-maidens began to appear with golden ewers for carrying water from the pond to the Princess's bath. Prince Suthon therefore made a prayer asking the gods to bear witness to his invocation, namely, if he was going to be united with his wife once more, then he prayed the gods to cause the water ewer of one of those maidens to be so heavy that she could not lift it up without his assistance. One of the maiden, finding her water jar so heavy, shouted aloud for help from her companions and so Prince Suthon made his presence known to her, and helped her lifting the pot out of the water and, while so doing, slipped his ring into the water in the pot.

As Princess Manora was pouring water on her body, lo! her little finger caught something which, upon closer scruting, proved to be nothing but her beloved spouse's ring which she deposited with the Anchorite on her way back. She was so pleased with this turn of the event, that she asked the water-carrier about the whole affair.

Manora   — And now, where is that man who gave you help?

Water Carrier   — He is somewhere around the lotus pond now.

Manora   — Don't let any body know about this. That man is my long-lost Prince, take these clothes, perfumes and ornaments to him so that he will be properly clad.

Manora then sallied forth to announce the glad tidings to her parents who marvelled at the power and perseverance of Prince Suthon and they immediately sent for him. The King praised his wondrous exploits and the Prince told the King thus:

"If Your Majesty want to test my skill in archery, then please order that seven palmyra palm-trees be placed in a row four cubits apart. Then place beside each palm trunk, a figwood board of three cubits thick, beyond the fig boards let seven stone pillars be placed and, in between, let fourteen plates of metals namely seven of iron and seven of copper, of each one cubit in thickness, be piled side. Beyond that let seven more bullock carts, fully laden with sand be placed side by side and through all these I shall let fly my arrow."

The King put him to this test and found his vaunting true-nay, more than true because the arrow cleft through the ocean, through Mount "Chakravan"[1] to the awe and dewilderment of gods and Kinnaras alike. Notwithstanding this, however, King Tumarat remarked: "There is stall a solid stone bench in my palace here which requires no less than one thousand stalwart men to raise it up one inch, do you think you can manage that?"

The King hardly finished his sentence when Prince Suthon rushed to the stone bench and lifted it up bodily.

"With all these to your credit, do you think you can pick out your wife from among other damsels here?" asked the King. "I think I can" replied the Prince, when suddenly he was almost frozen with fright as seven identical maidens began to file pass him,

---

1. Cakravala

"Take away your wife then" said the king. In his last resort, Suthon invoked Indra's help and behold! a golden insect was suddenly seen to fly three times around a maiden's head before finally alighting on it. Suthon seized her arm and proclaimed her his wife in the presence of all. The King and Queen bestowed blessings on the long-separated couple and the whole concourse joined in the jubilation, and the Prince and Princess lived happily until the end of their alloted span.

———

ASNI AND KOKILA

Long, long ago, when the gods and goddesses lived so near to human beings, it was told that Uma the wife of Siva, came once a year on the full moon of the 12th month to visit the water fall of Sa—barb.[1] It so happened that once, in that occasion, a hermit offered her the wondrous coral flowers........ When the ceremonial dance, so perfectly performed by her devotees was over, the Goddess, being so pleased with them, threw them these flowers, two of them quarelled........ And Uma said unto them:

"Behold, my angels, you behave yourselves just like mortals, so with them you shall stay. You shall be born in this land called Suvannapum[2] You shall live, love and suffer. Unless you taste the bitter joy of sacrificing your own sweet love, you shall not come back into our blissfull heavens again........

So both angels came to the earth, in the land of Suvannapum. One became a rich fisherman's only daughter; she is not such a beauty, but as once, in heaven, she used to sing to the gods, she is bestowed with a lovely, soothing, appealing voice, so that her

---

1. Sa-barb = to wash away the sin. A waterfall in Chantaburi.
2. Suvarna bhumi

parents called her Kokila.[1] The other was born to a poor owner of a pine-apple orchard. She was born in the throes of the strongest tempest they remembered ....Three big trees were destroyed in their compound. So they gave her the name of Asni.[2] Asni was a picture of delight; so charming and so graceful she was in her own sweet way.

Both girls grew up together in the same village. Kokila was spoiled by Fortune: Her parents were rich; herself, though not a beauty, had such a caressing voice that they granted her all she asked, While Asni had to work hard, helping her poor parents in their pine-apple plantation, knowing little of the joy of being loved, pampered and admired.

It was the rainy season, but for weeks and weeks, there had been no rain. Crops, fruits, vegetables perished all around....The Elders of the community held council: They then come to the conclusion that there must be a propiation to Phra Pirun[3] for rain.

All the villagers came to the open space in front of Asni's house. While the elderly ones sat around jars of arrack, laughing and drinking, the younger ones performed the ceremony: They put a black female cat in a basket attached to a rope, tied to a pole carried over the shoulders of two boys. The cat is very well decorated. They marched it around the place, beating drums, laughing, singing:

---

1   a bird with a beautiful voice like the Chardonnuret.
2. lightning   3. Varuna

Good old Dame Cat....
You must ask for a cloudy sky,
You must ask for rain....
Let us ask for the lustral water to pour over
Good old Dame Cat....

They started to go around the fire, which they had lighted in the middle of the place, taking care that their right side was always nearest to the fire.[1] After three circumambulations, they set the cat free. And all the young girls performed the dance saluting and praising and asking forgiveness to the god of rain....

Among the audience was a strong, handsome man, just came back from the metropolis, his name was Manop. This man, like the others, couldnot take his eyes off Asni: so graceful, so light, so sublime was her dance: for in her previous incarnation, she used to dance to the Wife of Siva....

Manop went up to Asni's parents, as soon as the dance was over; and after inquiring them about their health and their work as befitted the occasion, he discreetly inquired about Asni, who was his play-mate.

Father — Asni, Asni, come and pay respects to your elder brother[2]

---

1. the clockwise way.
2. It is quite usual for a girl to address a friend as elder brother or elder sister, as a sign of intimacy or friendliness

Asni	— Oh, elder brother, How you've changed, I can hardly recognise you.
Manop	— High time for me to come back, then? But I, I never forget you, younger sister Asni.
Father	— Manop, Manop, you have a golden tongue, I'm afraid many a young girls' heart will be broken, soon."

The father and Manop laughed, looking at Asni. She looked downcast for a second, joined in the laughter and simply said:

"Father, I must go and help Mother putting the rice in the bowls. Are you coming to join the fishermen or would you like me to bring it up to you here?"

Father	— "We'll be down with them won't we, Manop?

Asni ran towards the group of women without waiting for an answer, knowing quite well that Manop's keen eyes were follwing her.

Manop said: "My Uncle, you must know that if I speak sweetly, it is only with Asni that I speak thus, I'm not using this language with every girl, I assure you..../

Kokila came up to join them, and soon they are all dancing, laughing, drinking and frolic-making, around the big fire where some were cooking rice in bamboo, some cooking the small salted fish and some smoking quietly the lotus-wrapped cigars.

Kokila was rather vexed that Asni should become the centre of attraction, this evening. But soon, her sombre humour passed away, for with Asni's suggestion, her father asked her to sing, and having sung once before the gods, her voice sounded heavenly; and she herself forgot her own misery....

Manop loved Asni so much that he did not even notice the golden voice of Kokila. And that did not please the latter at all. For Manop was afterall a handsome man, and Kokila was anything but inhuman. But, one day Fate brought him to her.... Kokila was sitting on a rock. while Manop without looking up, threw the rope to tie his boat to a tree and hurt her. Manop heard a woman's cry. He ran to her, seeing Kokila he asked; "Oh, Kokila, did I hurt you ?"

Kokila did not answer, she did not look up, but put both her hands on her bleading ankle. Manop was anxious. He knelt down by her side, tore the edge of his cloth-belt, saying: "Poor sister, let me help you."

He then gingerly and coyly took her foot on his knee saying: "Pardon", and carefully wrapped the ankle with trembling hands.

Still Kokila did not say a word. Trembling, a little herself, thrilled, she looked at his brown torso, his big firm muscle, and unconsciously smiled. Having finished, Manop looked up, meeting her joyous eyes, he laughed a little awkwardly and asked : "Feeling better?"

The girl shook her head disapprovingly: " Manop, you should not touch a woman's feet. You know it will spoil all the manly glory which resides within you, especially as you have all those amulets around your neck."

Manop put his hand to the golden chain, touching the talisman and the small figures hung to it, then he shrugged his broad shoulders.

Manop   — But you are hurt by my carelessness, younger sister.

Kokila   — I should have warned you; but, listen, elder brother, promise me that you will go to renew the charm of this amulet of yours this very night....And now, let me salute you at your feet and thus bring back your luck."

Kokila joined her hands and brought them to the very ground at Manop's feet. He stooped down hastily and caught her hands in his. She laughed gaily and he realised for the first time that her voice was like a silver bell.............

* * * * *

O most happy Wife of Siva, stop your game.... Let not their young hearts be burnt of such ardent love. Let Manop see his way clearly. He is human, so he must not be so tempted. Life is so full of misery. If you cannot spare them Love, the source of all suffering on this earth, give him back to Asni...: She is his and he is hers: for she loves him first... But oh, that is not a solution: Where there is love, there is suffering. O, Uma, Uma, take them back to your Heaven ......

* * * * *

Manop, at the entreaty of Kokila's father, was now working with the fishermen. He was thus near to the lovely voice, in spite of himself. True and faithful was his love for Asni. But alas, Manop was born on Monday, and according to the oriental belief. he was of the opinion that ".... beauty should be scorn'd in none, though truly served but one...." His love for Asni was like the sea-moss: though its roots were firmly attached to the rocks, its leaves quivered a little as the currents passed by. He cheriched Asni dearly, but when Kokila spoke to him in her goddess-like tone, he couldnot help admiring her.... Manop was a fine strong man and Kokila loved to be admired by every one....

Asni saw all this threatning shadows, but her faith in Manop was so strong that she averted herself of suspicion, only watching and aching silently.... And besides, she had so much work to do: her parents were so old, and she held so much responsibility, that she had no time to linger on her own grievance,

One day as she was cutting down the pine-apples, she came across a golden one hidden among the leaves. The whole village was agog with this discovery, and they all advised her to send it to the King. But her father said: "Asni, they give us a sound advise: the King might reward us and that might help us out of our misery........But I know you like this fruit, it is so lovely. Keep it then, my child. Keep it, my little Mouse[1] your parents cannot afford to give you anything so lovely.

But, Asni knew she must not keep it, so with the fisherman it went to the King....And when they came back, they had the royal order to take Asni to the court........

* * * * *

O, Goddess of Fate, have mercy upon this beautiful girl. You should not "bring the meat to the Tiger's mouth"....as says the old Siamese adage. She is unhappy enough, being so far away from Manop, leaving her with such a temptation as Kokila. So sad, so lonely, in the cage of gold....The King sent costly gifts to her parents; for great was her charm, but greater the King's desire....Her grief and anxiety were beyond description....But the King were gracious enough to wait for her consent....Weeks passed away, and Asni couldnot but beg him to let her go back to her pine-apple field.

1. Mouse is an affectionate term for children. Sometimes, when speaking with parents, children call themselves "Mouse" instead of using the word " I "

But, one day, the time of her expiation was drawing to its end the King called her to his presence and she said unto him:

"My Lord, it is the most desirable wish of every woman to be your handmaid. And I'm no exception to the rule....But, you see, my Lord. I've vowed to be loyal...."

King — But you are not married, you do not know what you call Love, and no man has the right to own you, my child.

Asni — But I love him, and by the right of love I own him. I own the man I love, and every woman, be her a slave or a queen, my Lord....

King — This is a very clever pretext, but if it is my pleasure....

Asni — My most noble Lord owner of my life, may I say a word? You have the whole kingdom....

King — Shut your pretty mouth....You know my wish....

Kokila — Most noble Lord above my humble head, spare my virtue. I know the sweet happiness of love, but I also taste the bitterness of its deception. You have a Queen, my Lord. What a woman had done unto me, I swear to heaven that I will not do it to another woman.

King	— If I insist?
Kokila	— I shall end my life rather than commit a sin which I shall have to go through again in the next life. God is my witness, my Lord.

It happened that the royal fancy was over and the King ordered that Asni should be sent back to her village.

But when she came back to her place she could hardly believe her own eyes. The house and the farm were gone, her parents died....lots of things had changed since the last appearence of the decoits they told her. Asni did not even care to hear the rest........ She left them and walked straight ahead........ "O, my brother, I have but you. Please, Manop docome to me, O, please." Unconsciously, she ran towards the fisherman's village. The sun has just disappeared over the dark sea, only its rays lighted the sky on glorious hues. Then she saw a man coming towards her; he must be drunk, the way he walked and talked to himself.

Asni	— Can you remember me, Friend?
Friend	— Me, me?....Now let me think, what's your name?
Asni	— Asni! daughter of Uncle Tarn, do you remember now?
Friend	— Asni? Asni! ....Oh, yes, Manop....
Asni	— Yes, Manop Manop how is he? Where is he? please, please, do tell....

Friend	— He is doing fine, my lass.... but Kokila is dying, I suppose: He does not care for her.
Asni	— O, Friend, tell me all.
Friend	— There is nothing to tell. Manop loves you and still waits for you.
Asni	— Then what's wrong with Manop and Kokila?
Friend	— Kokila has refused everybody.... she loves the god-like friend of mine. But though he is weak at times, he remains faithful to you and swears to your Father that as long as you live no other girl shall be his wife,
Asni	— Well Manop....
Friend	— So Kokila, her pride wounded, tried to hang herself, but they found her and saved her in time....I know the girl, she'll kill herself alright one day.

Asni did not wait to hear the rest. She ran straight ahead, laughing, feeling no fatigue, no hunger. There was a short-cut, a buffalo-sart track.... The earth was almost dark, but above, the azured sky was still clear and limpid, a few stars twinkled lonely in that immense serene space.

Asni jumped back with a sharp cry: She stumbled over something warm and sticky, something that was still, and yet quivering, making small yelping noise. She suppressed her fear, stooping down, she saw a dog; it must have been run over by a cart, quite recently: its body was still warm, six or seven puppies crawled and yapped around the dead beast ..

Asni staggered backward.... her heart was beating fast. She wiped her feet with dry leaves, then sat still, too frightened, too disgusted to move or to do anything.... She suddenly felt as though things were moving around her in a great swirl. Breathing deeply, she leaned back against the tree; she saw the sky become a deeper blue and stars increase in number; the mountain breeze was blowing her hair over her face. She brushed her hair away, moving her head up at the same time.... Then, she felt the pang of loneliness, horrors, fears, fatigue, hunger, desperation, rushed into her whole self....

"O, Uma, my Goddess, call me back, take me back to thy bosom, Life is but sadness, I can count my hours of joy....O, Manop, Manop, my own, I love you, O, love you more than I can tell. Please come to me, do come to me, I'm dying....

Then, she raised her head to look at the sky, she realised all of a sudden, the emptiness of life, and she said to herself: "We will cease the battle. Kokila, you can have Manop, dear. Let us not be enemies, for what I do unto you this life, you will do unto me in the next."

The cries of the puppies brought back her to reality. She picked them up, hoping to bring them to the house she saw yonder. This will be her last kind deed on earth. Then she would go to the rocks that stretch in to the sea. Once dead, nobody would see the ugliness of her lifeless form.... The wood was quite dark ' and Asni had to fumble her way under the dim lights from the stars....

The little creatures ceased to cry, as they lay in her arms. She felt less miserable and walked slowly, watching her step. When she came up to the back fence, the odour of boiled rice set her thinking again.... Tears streamed down her pale cheeks. In a second, she saw her father, her mother sitting at the door of their house looking at the pot of boiling rice at the fire. She heard someone say: "Thou shalt not kill thyself, for thou shalt thus be repeating the suicide in the next live to come....

Asni thought she called out Manop's name and without knowing she let go the puppies.... Manop, Manop, brother dear.... But she felt a sharp pain on her neck, and all was darkness to her........

The owners of the house heard strange noises: they thought some beasts of prey must have come to attack their domestic animals and so they shot an arrow into the dark. It is better to be on the safe side: You never can tell. Evil spirits often take the form of human beings at this hour that separates the day from the night and come to harm the nwelyborn child in the house. So not only did they put thorns around their house, but also chased evil spirit by shouting or scaring them away with bolts of arrows.

People came out of the house, armed, carrying lighted torches with them. They saw the beautiful maiden lying still, dead among the puppies. But, lo, yonder on the peak of the Sabarb Mountain, behold, there was a strange spectacle: a strange effulgence of lights floated over the high peak, strange forms moved around in circle. They saw beautiful rays of lights and heard most beautiful strange music. And behold, in the midst of these ethereal beauties, they saw a maiden dancing so skillfully, so gracefully, that they thought of Asni. Her face seemed to be familiar to them, they looked at the body....Lo, it was no more there....But as they watch the scene it grew dimmer and dimmer, until it disappeared altogether in the sky....

It was Uma, Wife of Siva who came to receive the soul of Asni, her favorite, to take her back to heaven so that she might once more enjoy the ever-lasting joy and happiness.

Printed at Don Bosco Technical School & Orphanage
Ruam Chai lane - Bangkapi - Bangkok
M. Gomiero Printer and publisher
14-9-54